Swapna Das has lived in the UK for more than 30 years. She is an avid reader and writing is one of her main interests. Swapna has studied English literature at college. She has travelled extensively and enjoys observing different cultures. Swapna follows national and global issues, and she has organised several fund-raising events (with support from family and friends) for UK charities. Watching comedy shows and documentary movies keeps the author occupied in her spare time. She is also an amateur photographer and is always on the lookout for a good click. Swapna has a special fondness for cooking and spending time in the kitchen when time permits. The author has published two books to her credit – *A String of Pearls* (2016) and *The Forgotten People* (2019).

Swapna Das

SHRISTI: CREATION

AUSTIN MACAULEY PUBLISHERS™

LONDON • CAMBRIDGE • NEW YORK • SHARJAH

A CIP catalogue record for this title is available from the British Library.

ISBN 9781035868292 (Paperback)
ISBN 9781035868308 (ePub e-book)

www.austinmacauley.com

First Published 2024
Austin Macauley Publishers Ltd®
1 Canada Square
Canary Wharf
London
E14 5AA

Table of Contents

Planets of the Gods

"The immense space of the bejewelled dark sky
Is the dwelling of the dominant Gods."
The several celestial bodies in its ring
Adorn the pathway to heaven and to Lords.

Small Mercury spinning around like a top
Around the sun is a frenzy picture to behold.
Its proximity to the Sun God,
And swathed in heat, makes it
The smallest and fastest dot.

Like a top spinning in the opposite direction,
Venus is a proud and bright hot ball of fire and motion.
Her name bears resemblance to love and beauty,
As she is the only female deity in the hall of fame and
devotion.

Earth is the third rock in the solar ring,
Gracefully gliding around the sun in 365 days.
It boasts of creatures big and small,
And also of the blue waterways.
The sphere prides itself as the fifth largest sibling
In the family of planets and the Milky Way.
It has many treasures to attract the desire of others
And the adventures of Aliens from beyond the bay.

A red planet called Mars dots the night sky
And has a thin atmosphere the family knows in the sly.
Also similar physical features of Earth and Moon
Make it the most researched planet for the human mind.

The size of Jupiter is the talk of the Milky Way,
Its dusty storm and many moons give it an exclusive place.
It is the largest planet of the solar system,
And is placed fifth in the planetary loop.
Jupiter was the main God of the Romans,
And is visible to the naked eye and Kings.

With its icy rings, Saturn is an inimitable planet.
It rivals with Jupiter in size and moons,
And has many planetary rings to claim.
The Romans celebrated him as a God
Of Abundance and Wealth,
And spectacles as bright and close to Earth
In the still night sky.

Uranus has a very strange rotation!
Unlike other planets,
For it spins on its side at a 90-degree motion.
It is the seventh planet in the solar ring,
Therefore not a bright star to shine.
But the planet is revered in Greek Mythology
As a God to worship and realise it's divine.
Lonesome Neptune is distant from the Sun,
For it is the eighth planet on the run.
It is the fourth largest and lonely planet,
With its smallest gas giants.

Neptune has Triton as its only moon and companion,
So lonesome it is that it has no warmth to embrace.

Pluto is still considered the ninth planet of the Solar System,
It is the dwarf planet of the family,
And has five known moons as a claim.
But only recently it became known as a Planet name.

****

Water World

From the mountain top,
She began her silent journey
Towards the land below.
As she meandered through
The plains and forests,
And remained unaffected,
To write her own story.

She journeyed relentlessly
For a place in the ocean,
And to experience the wonders of the
Blue paradise,
To be part of a world,
And to see its glory,
And to make a home
In the mighty water world.

****

The waterway glided through the vast land
To witness the many lives
Of creatures great and small.
And saw the many beauties of the
Promised land,
And birds singing in nature's hand.

She became a stream at a certain point,
But remained a force to reckon with,
As she voyaged on the fertile land
With beauty and grace.

She recovered her original form
And gushed down the steep slope.
As the sound of the rushing river
Caught the attention of the lone soul,
He stopped to see the magnificence
Of the mighty water force,
Streaming down the hills of hope.
He sat on the banks for a few moments,
To drink in the beauty of
Nature's marvel of waterway.

****

From a distance, she could smell
The air of places far and aloof.
She knew that the water fed
The many farmlands of a few.
The small fish bobbed up and down
As the river wound its way,
While the mighty bear
Stared at the waterway,
Seeking its prey.
The edge was covered in tall trees,
As branches dropped in its sideways.
The humming bird looked for a place
To make its nest and keep it safe.

The deer in the forest sprinted fast,
To quench its thirst
From the running watercourse,
And stands by to gaze without any remorse.
She flips her tail to chase the fly
And looks up to see
The sapphire sky.

****

Many forces of nature beleaguered her journey,
But she was not afraid.
For she continued to rush down the hill
In a fearsome way.
The stormy sky threatened the land,
And rain was not far behind.
For it lashed down on the green meadow,
To quench the parched land.
At one point the sun was intense
On the farmland and beyond,
And not a sound could be heard,
As everything was silent,
By chance everyone was gone.

The cattle on the fields mooed aloud,
As the brook rushed forward,
To seek her onward journey,
To the seas beyond.
Her gait bent left and right,
On the flat land of peace.
She never forgot to bless the earth,

Also in her moment of ease.
She silently watched with awe,
The wonders of the life of all.
The small cricket dancing on the grass,
The sunflower swaying gracefully,
And The bumblebee buzzing away merrily.

She noticed the blue sky above,
With streams of small broken clouds,
And the seagull prancing around,
Like a child in a playground.
The river's attention was never broken,
As she watched life pass by.
The small details of the land,
Was always in her mind.

The sounds of the gushing brook
Broke the silence of the night,
As bats and owls sang in harmony,
As if to join her onward journey,
Down the ravines and lands of pine.
Her long journey through the landscape,
Was full of spirit and delight,
For she was the life giver
Of everything dense and light.

Spring was not far behind,
As daffodils adorned the fields,
And the many birds squeaked in trees.
She noticed the sunflower land,
Dancing in the breeze as if in romance.

The stream kept moving forward,
As if someone was waiting in hand.
The rushing waters of the stream
Made a rhythmic sound of love and peace,
As if the land nearby was in comfort and ease.

The summer sun dazzled the sky,
She noticed with her open eyes.
The sunrays sparkled on the water,
Like diamonds in the daylight.
A grazing cow mooed loudly,
To let the river know her might.
And by chance a white flower,
Dropped on the flowing tide.

****

The auburn-coloured leaves of trees
Dropped graciously on the land,
To let the river know the season of warmth was over,
That the night sky would be long and cooler.
She watched the changing season,
With awe and admiration.
The mighty drift kept her going towards the ocean.
She did not stop at any point,
As she was on a mission,
To join the forces of the great big sea,
And experience the wonder of the waterscape.
Winter was not far behind,
And there was a chill in the air.
The birds had stopped singing,

And they returned to their nest early,
To sleep in the comfort of the night.
Occasionally the rushing river,
Heard the owl hoot suddenly,
A reminder that she was awake,
Keeping a watchful eye on her prey.

As she passed the many farmlands,
The water was slow to run,
And the surface was a bed of icicles,
But the current below was fearsome.
The water below flowed relentlessly,
Without any reason to stop.

After a long journey on land,
The river could smell the ocean's air.
As she wandered the last lap,
With confidence and delight,
She saw a vast blue sea from a distance,
And excitedly she told herself,
"This is my mission,
To be in union with the ocean.
Suddenly she joined the vast water land,
She was delighted to be in union.
The waves in the bay,
Smacked the surface with white froth,
And the seagulls hovering above,
Looking for fish during the day."

****

The Mermaid's Plea

The mermaid watched in silence
From afar on the ocean's surface.
She observed with curiosity
Children playing on the sand
With their tender hands.
She looked around with curiosity,
Her tail swaying gently in the sea.
She wondered for a moment
As she watched the elderly couple
Feeding birds in the sand.

She leaped back deep in the ocean,
Swimming rapidly to ask questions
And seek answers from the God of the Sea.
She whirled for a good hour
And reached a cave covered in green
In the calm waters below.
The mermaid briefly stopped for a moment
Outside the large cave,
Lowered her tail, and glided gently
Alone with her tail.

With reverence and awe,
The mermaid entered the abode of the God.
Vishnu, seated on a decorated throne
With his hands on his knee
And deep in thought,
The mermaid stopped in front of the God,
Looked at him with wonder and a nod.
For she had witnessed many scenes
On the beach by the sea
And yearned for answers from Him,
For she believed in his divinity.
"What brings you to see me, Nerida?"
Vishnu asked with an air of authority.
He looked calm and amused
As he saw the audience of small fish
Gently glide by the golden-tailed fish.
They too looked at her in amazement
As Nerida looked confused
And her tail tossed from side to side
In the calmness of the silent world.
The mermaid looked directly at the God
And spoke about questions in her mind,
As she pleaded for answers from Him.
"The water world we live in is dark;
Why is it so?
The sun shines bright on land,
Why is it so?
What makes people laugh and cry?
Why do we not have the same moods?
Children play happily in the sand,
Not aware of the dangers of the sea.

What keeps them safe and free?
The river has witnessed life on land
Before she joined the sea.
Did you know her destiny?
I see four-legged animals play in the sand
As people laugh and clap their hand.
The birds move in a circle in the blue sky,
Waiting to catch their prey in the land.
What gives humans so much pleasure,
To enjoy life in their leisure?
I watched a group of people sing in joy,
As if their life is a plaything like a toy.
The big ocean waves hit the land,
And return to sea in a movement so grand.
Oh Vishnu, god of the ocean, please explain
the life and time and space I see?
I implore you to give the answers I seek.
What is the reason for the changing seasons?
For us creatures in the sea do not know the reason?
Multitude of interrogations cross my mind
As I watch in awe the life on land
And the passing of time as I stand."

As she spoke, Matsyakanya was a sight to behold,
Her golden hair draped in seaweeds
She picked up on her return to the deep sea.
Her blue fish companion sprinted in the water,
Looking at both the God and the mermaid
As if contemplating an answer any moment.
The bottomless sea seems calm and quiet,
The eerie silence was never broken.

The sea plants swayed gracefully in the tide
As Aaoka gracefully swung side by side.
Patiently she waited for an answer from Him,
As she watched Vishnu deep in thought and nod.
She looked sideways at her companion,
His blue fin dancing in the dark ocean.
Nine white flowers caught the mermaid's attention
As she reeled towards the slender tree,
She was in admiration of the blooms
And wondered if the flowers also reared on land.

Aaoka waited long for an answer,
But Vishnu was deep in sleep.
He twitched his ears occasionally,
And let the mermaid know
He was listening.
The ocean darkness, the silence was strange,
But life was not still and creepy.
The mermaid looked beyond her master
And saw the penguin swim near her.
The oceanic flowers were in full bloom
As the wildflowers swayed gently in tune.

The God's face was somber but kind,
His powerful look spoke her mind.
His long hair floated on his eyes
As he gently pushed it aside.
The gold Chakra on his right hand
Reflected his power of the sea,
And the mermaid was in awe of this.
He felt the sudden surge of energy

As he lifted his right hand
To greet the beautiful mermaid.
He was deep in thought,
And He remembered her words and looked lost.
She waited good-naturedly for Him to speak,
But Vishnu was not in a hurry
To give answers to her queries.
He looked left and right,
And watched the shoal of fish pass by.
His right hand was strong and able
To hold the mighty trident.
He raised the left hand
To pick the flower on his feet.
The looks had the signs of a gentle soul,
And his piercing smile had stories untold.

The tall slim body sat on the throne,
Showing power and control of the
World below he owned.
After a break of several minutes,
The God of the vast sea spoke.
The mermaid looked eager
To hear what he told.
"Your questions are innocent,
But answers are complex
To be understood by you and all,"
Said Vishnu calmly to Aaoka.
She looked at him with excitement
And floated gently towards his seat.
The mermaid was happy to hear him speak.
The God continued in his gentle tone,

"The world you see with your eyes
Is more than you can comprehend.
The water world is different in many ways
As it narrates the existence of the waterways.
The life you see in the ocean
Is the life they have preferred.
And the life you see on land
Is also the life they have chosen.
To compare the life on land and sea
Would be a mistake,
For it is different in so many ways.
It celebrates its own existence.
The blue sky is where the heaven is,
The blue sea is peaceful and still."
With a pensive nod, the mermaid spoke,
"Why is it different on land and sea,
Why one has to swim in the sea,
Whilst humans walk the land free?
Why do humans walk upright,
And we glide in the deep sea?"
The lord was listening intently
And paused to look around.
He closed his eyes again
So that he could contemplate again.
As the still water brushed his cheek.

The water was calm and silent,
But the ocean was full of life and zest.
Both God and Aaoka were
Deep in thought and feelings.
They looked at each other again

And smiled with a curious look.
They knew that all answers were not known,
But questions need to be asked too.
The giant whale passed by lazily,
And side by side swam the large turtle.
He looked sideways to observe the scene,
But oblivious of the conversation.
The water jungle was full of life,
And the hush of the water world
Resonated with the tides.
All creatures great and small
Coexisted in the sublime world
Without any rancor or hate,
For the peace of its surroundings
Was central to all life in the ocean.

The wisdom words spoken were uplifting,
But not clear to all listening.
Few creatures lifted their tails and ears,
Whilst others pondered for many years.
The bright sun had gone to sleep,
The ocean was calm and serene.
But Matsyakanya was still curious
About life on land and sea.
Vishnu did not speak any longer
As he watched the creatures in wonder.
She swam up to the surface of the sea

And noticed the dark shadows of the night
Cast its magic on the sleeping land.
She could hear the waves crash against the shore,

And a few birds tucking their plumes in the nest.
The mermaid's golden tail twitched a bit
When she saw the lonely dog on the beach.
She wondered how he came there
And thought maybe his master

Had abandoned him there.
She looked far beyond the shore
And saw the large trees standing tall
In the quietness of the winter land.

The night was long and still,
But the mermaid was awake as she looked
At the nearby hill.
The lonely dog sat still on the beach,
Looking towards the star in the sky.
He barked a few times
As if he recognized his master's voice
Telling him to sleep.

The few words of wisdom of the God
Answered some of her queries.
Aaoka twirled peacefully in the ocean,
Remembering the words of Vishnu
And added her own thoughts,

"Life is a mystery never to be solved
By humans and all.
It is a blessing that the world
Breathes life in all its forms,
And to glorify the moment
That touches the soul
With gratitude and love."

****

The Percussionist

At a very young age, Nipa was a boy of remarkable qualities. Born to a humble Bengali family, Nipa harboured dreams that did not include any academic ambition. Instead, music was his first love, and he played the beats of a drum whenever and wherever he had the opportunity. From the very start, he understood the beats of a tabla or a khol, and it seemed he was a natural percussionist. Frequently, he would play the tabla at the request of his friends at the local club, mesmerising them with the sound of the taal (beats) he produced, prompting them to join in with synchronised claps with every beat.

Within a short passage of time, the young boy's talent became the centre of discussions in the local community. Meanwhile, Nipa's parents took keen interest in their son's natural talent, and over time, Nipa's father, Jogen, decided to save money so that he could send his son to a tabla master (guru) to learn the finer skills of the art. In between attending to school homework, the teenager would often be asked to play khol (mridangana) at the nearby temple for special occasions, never missing the opportunity to display his skill and happily obliging the devotees. The young boy grew up to be a handsome, well-mannered adult. Jogen had saved enough money to send his son to a special music school owned by a famous tabla player in Kolkata.

On his first day at the school, Nipa was somewhat nervous at the prospect of meeting the famous tabla player, Naren, who was well-known in the country. His anxiety was soon overcome as he entered the big hall and noticed a senior man seated on the floor with a tabla in front of him. Nipa realised he was not the only student in the room; a few other young men were also present. The guru's assistant brought the tablas and placed the pairs in front of the pupils as they looked on nervously. The daya (right-hand tabla) and baya (small left-hand tabla) were placed in front of Nipa. The room was silent except for the sound of the master's voice, the learners waiting patiently for instructions from their guru.

Naren spoke softly and gently to his students, reminding them that he was strict about lessons but also friendly and approachable. He assured the young men not to worry if they missed any beat. With a few words spoken, the guru and his students began to play the first beats on their instrument. The same taal was repeated for a few minutes until they all played in synchronicity, and the master felt satisfied. With each symmetrical beat accompanied by sitar music, the room reverberated with the sounds of a forgotten era. The guru and his disciples followed each taal with delight and sincerity, and the music produced caught the attention of the public. Naren's neighbours always felt privileged to hear him play the tabla with his students and always looked forward to the teaching sessions.

Two years of intense training by his guru resulted in the making of a new confident Nipa. He played the instrument with ease and mastered the art of jugalbandhi (duet) with his musicians. Jogen and his wife, Nirmala, were proud parents as their only child excelled in his art, speaking of his achievement to family and friends. Nipa's career as a percussionist flourished under the tutelage of his guru. Most of Nipa's invitations to play the tabla at functions came with the blessings of the maestro, and within a short period, Naren recommended his most proficient student to accompany famous vocalists at functions. Nipa's financial situation improved dramatically, and at his young age, he was able to afford most of the luxuries for the family. Jogen worked less at the factory and instead engaged in promoting his son's career. The family was happy and settled, and Nipa's contribution was acknowledged by his parents. At the age of 25, Nipa married his childhood sweetheart – Debi. The daughter-in-law was accepted as a family member, and Debi and her family's relationship with Nipa's family grew from strength to strength. The couple were soon blessed with a son and then, two years later, with a daughter. After five years, the family welcomed the couple's third child, another daughter.

The second child, Bittu, was not of good health, and Debi was always troubled about this, seeking medical help whenever Bittu was ill. Nipa was busy with his career and often had to travel outside to play at events. As she grew, Bittu's health settled; at the age of four, she was inquisitive and playful, particularly missing her father when he had to travel to another city and stay overnight. Therefore, Bittu availed of every opportunity to be with her father. She observed him closely during his practice sessions at dawn. The beats of the tabla in the early morning served as a wakeup call for the small child. She would wake up and tiptoe to the ground floor to observe her father do riyaz (practice) on the percussion. Bittu was fascinated as she watched Nipa through the hanging door curtain, observing every movement of her father's palm and fingers on the tablas – Nipa would take out the daya and baya tablas from his large blue jute bag and place them on the floor near the large bay window. The morning sunlight filled the room and the tabla beats could be heard by the neighbours. Nipa practised the percussion instrument with his eyes closed and with sincerity; Bittu would push aside the long door curtain just to have a glimpse of her father. She watched and listened with amazement to the perfection of her father's craft on the tablas. The little girl grew up with these blessed memories of the mornings with her father and cherished every moment of her innocent experience.

Professionally, Nipa as a percussionist became famous and was much sought after for performances with well-reputed contemporary classical vocalists. He accompanied many of them to celebrated events, and the young performer became popular with his repertoire of tabla beats. He had the skill to match every musical instrument with his beats and would keep the audience captivated and entertained. His success was equally matched with simplicity and modesty, and on many occasions, he was the main attraction for any event.

On an early winter morning, Nipa readied to leave home to perform at a function outside his city. The journey would take him seven hours, so Debi packed food and a water bottle for her husband. He said goodbye to his family, and Bittu, in particular, was excited and hugged her father with a broad smile and wide-open eyes. He arrived at the venue in advance and found a quiet place to practise for the evening event, which would start in a couple of hours. The open-air event attracted a very large crowd, with music enthusiasts from the nearby towns also present. Nipa observed the large crowd through the veil of evening mist and felt a little nervous, as he had never performed in front of such a large gathering. However, he gathered courage and confidence and waited for the big moment of reckoning. After the organisers made the announcements, the musicians were introduced on the stage, and Nipa took his place on the left side of the vocalist Moloy, an exponent of Indian classical music. By this time, the crowd became silent as they waited expectantly to listen to the musical performance on stage. The concert started with an invocation to Goddess Saraswati. Moloy's deep voice rendered the ragas with utmost precision and skill; the musicians, including Nipa, accompanied the vocalist with their range of styles and skills; all eyes were on Nipa when the moment came for him to showcase his range of tabla beats to match Moloy's rendition, and both artists performed a masterpiece duet. The timely and skillful rendition of the vocalist and the tabla player invited the audience to clap in joy and devour every moment. The jugalbandhi (duet) lasted for ten minutes, and the audience's raptures echoed in the distance; it was the highlight of the evening.

After the success of the programme, many admirers attempted to reach Nipa and congratulate him; he was seen surrounded by men and women taking autographs and photos. The large crowd of more than two hundred admirers with Nipa didn't go unnoticed by Moloy, who stood at the corner of the stage speaking to a handful of people. Occasionally, he would give a sly glance in the direction of the other crowd; for him, it was a moment of reckoning that Nipa was the star of the evening and not him. As a famous vocalist, the reality made Moloy green with jealousy, and he left the venue without speaking to Nipa. The crowd and the musicians dispersed late in the night. Nipa returned home a happy artist with audience admiration, pockets full of cash, gold rings, a camera, and fruit and fish. Moloy returned home empty-handed.

For several weeks, the incident made Moloy insecure, and he actively spread malicious lies about Nipa to other professional singers of the time. This was the manner in which he disguised his jealousy for Nipa's success and good reputation. The ill act of Moloy resulted in other musicians' insecurity to include Nipa in their functions, as they felt that they would also meet the same fate as Moloy. They covertly influenced event managers to not include Nipa in the group of musicians. Steadily, the shows and events became less and far in between for Nipa. Initially, he did not understand the reasons for the change in fortune; however, a few loyal friends in the music industry informed him of Moloy's malice and the impact on Nipa's music career. The young tabla player was disheartened and disillusioned with the sudden change in his life, as playing the tabla was not just his profession but also his passion for music. Many months passed, and Nipa was left behind in his career due to professional jealousy and insecurity of another fellow musician. However, he continued his early morning riyaz to acquire further skills on the tabla. Bittu was a few years older, and on the way to school, she would look at her father with admiration and love, telling him that he was the best tabla player in the world. This motivated Nipa to continue his musical journey with the tablas.

At the young age of 35, one afternoon before lunch, Nipa read the Gita for the last time and waited for lunch to be served. Suddenly, he felt uncomfortable and began to speak in a soft voice that he was experiencing chest pain. Bittu's grandmother was alone at home; however, she did not hear her son's call for help as she was busy in the kitchen. She came to the room after ten minutes and discovered her son's body on the bed; however, unaware that he had breathed his last, she called out her son's name. After repeated calls and with no response, she touched his body with a concerned look and realised that her beloved son had left the world with physical and emotional pain. She wept aloud, and the neighbours entered the room. They too realised the loss of their famous neighbour.

Nipa's sudden death impacted Bittu and the family; only Debi knew the dark truth about her husband's professional fate, which was the result of extreme professional jealousy and greed. In later years, many people questioned why Nipa's children never followed in his footsteps and learned music. On these occasions, Debi would be silent of the truth, for she knew that her talented husband died a broken man and a disillusioned musician.

****

Butterfly
(Prajapati)

The coloured wings of a creature so magnificent,
It is hard to define.
But it is one of the most loved ones
Of the Supreme creation,
For the world and mankind.
She spans her multi-coloured wings
On the flower and flies in the sky
In search of the Divine.
She holds her breath and spins her wings,
And invokes the sublime.
Butterfly, butterfly set me free,
To be like you and let me fly.

The red and yellow stripes on her wings
Tell the stories of colours.
The two dotted eyes on the brow
Search for her flowers and plants.
Yet she knows not that she is the one,
For the conception of beauty in the world.
She is the free soul of beauty and colour.
Butterfly, butterfly set me free,
To be like you and let me fly.

**************(Prajapati)*************

Bagan Bari
(Country House)

Rahul was suddenly awakened from his deep sleep by the sounds of rushing gallops and whispers outside. He looked at his bedside table and glanced at the small clock. It was late at night. He was perplexed and annoyed at the same time. He quickly left his bed and opened the bedroom window. He looked outside in the darkness for a few seconds and saw a few horses disappear in the night light, and heard the people mounted on them whisper to each other as they galloped away, leaving a cloud of dust behind. Their dark shadows diminished in size as they sprinted towards the other side of the town. Rahul's curiosity about the incident left him awake for a good thirty minutes, and finally, he fell asleep after drinking a glass of water.

Rahul Bagchi had served in Kaliput for a good eight years; his married life with Trisha was a happy one, and their son Deb was attending primary school. They lived with Rahul's parents, and extended family members lived nearby. The Bagchi household was a busy and noisy one. Deb spent most of his time with his grandparents, who would listen to his stories with interest and amusement. Deb had a good reputation in school and was admired at home for his storytelling skills. When he was very young, he would express his imagination by narrating incidents he pretended he had witnessed. Rahul was a busy doctor in the city and spent long hours treating his patients in different clinics. On a Wednesday, Rahul received an urgent telephone call from the head of the health department asking him to attend the office the next morning. Urgent matters had to be discussed and finalised. Therefore, on the following day, Rahul left for work earlier than his usual time and reached the health department building in the city well in advance. The building was not an impressive one but housed the most important health department, and the senior executives occupied the fifth floor of the building. The lift stopped on the fifth floor, and Rahul stepped out and walked in the direction of the director's office. He knocked on the door and entered the room. The director, Kanjilal, greeted him 'good morning, Rahul'. The men exchanged a smile and sat on a large sofa placed at the corner of the big room. "I understand I have been called today as a matter of urgency," Rahul queried. "Yes, Rahul, I have been asked to relocate you to Daliput on an urgent mission. I know it is short notice, but you are expected to be there in three days." Rahul was left speechless as he had not expected a relocation without any prior indication. He asked a few questions to Mr Kanjilal, who explained that Daliput was not very far from Kaliput; however, daily commuting would not be practical, therefore it would be convenient for Rahul to stay in the bungalow in Daliput. The large bungalow was owned by the department. Rahul was also informed about the reason for the sudden transfer to Diliput. He nodded his head even though he was surprised and left the room.

Daliput was a very small satellite town, a two-hour drive from Kaliput. The adjoining area had witnessed an increase in small factories and businesses. The population had also increased, and the small town had attracted the attention of migrant workers who took up menial jobs in the factories. A variety of small businesses had been launched, and this provided jobs to the migrant community, who lived in makeshift homes on the fringes of Diliput. They were not welcome in the small town, which had its share of very affluent people. The small migrant community arrived from different parts of India and spoke different languages, but their similar cultural and social habits united them. They were unified in their everyday struggles and hardships, but they were aware that jobs were not easy to find. Therefore, they settled for low-paid jobs in Daliput. The tinned houses they built was a testimony of their difficult existence. Sanitation was a big problem, and this resulted in poor health and safety, mainly for children. Men and women attended the menial jobs in the town in the day, whilst their children were looked after by their senior family members. The children did not attend any school, and their access to toys was nonexistent. The department of health had become aware of the small community and the health risks they posed. The absence of any medical care for the poor had come to the attention of the health department as they deliberated in their closed chambers to resolve the problem. The board had decided to relocate Rahul to Daliput, as he had experience of working outside Kaliput and had gained a good reputation as a competent community doctor.

One early afternoon, Rahul arrived at his new place of work with a suitcase in his hand and a bottle of water to quench his thirst in the hot summer. He was welcomed at the small bungalow at the end of the narrow road – from a distance, it looked impressive and caught the doctor's attention. The elderly man, Akash, opened the large gate, and the two men walked side by side to the front of the house. It was left unlocked, as Akash had come early to clean and tidy the place in preparation for the new occupant. The main hall was large and had a wooden beamed ceiling; the room was well furnished, and there were bookshelves near the window. Rahul looked around the room, and the smell of jasmine flower was prominent in the air – a white flower vase with the flowers occupied the corner table covered in lace tablecloth. Rahul was then shown the side room, which was to be his bedroom; it had a large bed with bedposts, and a mosquito net could be seen neatly tucked at the top. This reminded the doctor that the place was infested with the insect and for him to take precaution. The bedroom also had a wardrobe, table and chair, and a mirror on the wall. The room was large enough for Rahul to do his morning yoga, as he thought to himself. The senior man then guided Rahul outside the room, and they walked down a short passageway connecting the kitchen and the bathroom. At the end of the passageway, Rahul noticed a flight of stairs going down to the basement. He asked, "Is there a basement?" – "Yes," came the prompt reply from Akash.

Akash opened the door to a very large hall as he switched on the ceiling lights. The brightness of the room revealed an exquisite and magnificent collection of artwork, pottery, manuscripts, sitar, tabla, and other artefacts. He noticed that each item was carefully displayed on walls, shelves, tables. The four corners of the room had a large pillar painted in vibrant Indian motifs. The owner of the bungalow – a retired banker – had painstakingly collected the artworks over a period of time; he spent his retired life in the bungalow, admiring his collection and peacefully died a few years ago.

In his will, he had donated the bungalow to the health department with a condition that a doctor would be designated to work in the small town. The other condition was that only his family members and official dignitaries would have access to the magnificent chamber of artwork. Therefore, the basement hall was not open to the public as a museum but to be enjoyed by art enthusiasts. The young doctor walked around the large room, drinking in the beauty of everything that was on display. He guided himself and noticed the Madhubani wall painting, the Chao Masks, earthenware pottery including terracotta, the tarafdar sitar, a small jute carpet, sea shell garland, and many more. Rahul was overwhelmed with the secret finding in his bungalow and silently promised himself to explore the room further in his spare time. Akash explained to him that the key to the room would be left with the doctor and the duplicate key is in the possession of the banker's daughter, who visits occasionally to add to the collection or to simply spend time in the room.

The next day, the doctor's day began very early as he had to locate the temporary office where he would carry out his duties of seeing patients. The local people standing in a queue outside the building greeted Rahul. Before leaving his hometown, the officials had warned Rahul that there was an imminent outbreak of malaria in the region and for him to stockpile on medicines and equipment. This proved to be true in a few weeks, and the queue outside had grown in size, and the home visits had also increased. Rahul soon became a popular doctor in the community, and within a short time, he befriended a few loyal locals.

The following months witnessed several casualties due to the dreaded malaria. There was a water crisis also during the intense summer months, and this had exacerbated the problem. Most elderly frail people had succumbed to the disease, and the local hospital and the cemetery found it difficult to meet the needs of the time. Rahul, as an experienced and skilled doctor, felt helpless and sad that he was unable to ease the misery of the migrant community despite his earnest effort to do so. He wrote letters to his family frequently in order to offload a few of his sad experiences in the town. Months and weeks passed, and for Rahul, the time and difficulties seemed prolonged. However, during his moments of frustrations and vulnerability, he found comfort and solace in the company of the vast artwork collection in the basement of his bungalow. He would easily spend a couple of hours when he had free time to disconnect from the outside reality and enjoy the present moment.

Frequently, Rahul recalled his experience at the bungalow the first night and had speculated about the galloping horses. One day, he asked a senior member of the community about other locals. He was informed that a few wealthy men in their vicinity owned horses; they had questionable characters. The men would frequently visit the migrant community in search of young women as victims of their lust. The lustful men would forcefully pick up any woman they fancied and take them away mounted on the horses. The doctor listened with anger and surprise, and the next morning, he assembled a few young men and addressed them, "From tonight, two men will keep guard on the narrow streets and keep vigilance about late-night visitors; if any suspicious person enters the locality in the night, please come and call me even if it is late." Although this resulted in resentment in the adjoining wealthy area, the unpleasant incidents stopped suddenly, as there were rumours floating around that the doctor had high connections in the police force. This meant that if men were apprehended for their wicked act in the night, they would be arrested and sent to jail immediately. The fear of this had a positive impact on the safety of the women of the community.

39

****

Gandhari's Dream

He tiptoed on his tiny feet on the floor below,
Delighted with toys that were spread near the door.
Little Janu was always a happy and naughty boy,
But to his mother, he was the apple of her eyes.
She loved and cared for him like every mother would,
With a dream for her son that would fulfil her dream.
Janu's toys varied from a football with a map of his country,
To little hats of different colours, which he would
Wear with pride and a big smile.
He kicked the ball to and from with a loud scream,
As if to mean that the country was something to play with,
And be its king.

She taught him at a young age to lead the crowd,
But without any knowledge of leadership to feel proud.
He would listen to her sweet voice saying aspirational dreams,
For him to be the king of the land and seek esteem.
Gandhari worked hard to fulfil her vision,
As the years rolled on, Janu grew to be a teen.
Every advice from his beloved mother never ignored,
Whilst Gandhari planned her son's destiny,
To be the king.
Her yearning and longing for Janu's ambition
Seemed a distant dream, but she pursued it with keen interest.
She instructed her loyalists to nurture her dream,

As Janu would one day become the King.
Gandhari commanded a loyalty that many would envy,
But a few men preferred to be loyal to the country,
Rather than to the doting mother.
For many years the hard work for Janu did not bear fruit,
Many people thought of Gandhari as shrewd.
Nonetheless, she continued with her plan,
To fulfil her dream, as Janu was the chosen one,
To be the king.

In the meantime, the young man made many friends,
And loyalists too.
He changed and wore his coloured caps,
Depending on who is friend and who is foe.
Janu mimicked like a child even at twenty-four,
For he could do nothing better but to smile.
Knowledge of country and culture not known to him,
But his beloved mother dreamt for long for him,
To be the king.

She skilled him to think that the country was his,
And that one day the people would worship him,
Like a king.
Gandhari pursued with her dream for her son,
But didn't understand that people were not her own.
She told her followers to nurture the young man,
As if he was their own.
Despite her effort and shrewd ways,
Gandhari was unable to convince all,
That Janu was not the chosen one at all.
As a mother with a big dream,

Gandhari was always very keen for her son,
To be the king.
But his destiny was not meant,
For him to be the king.

****

The Masseuse

The early spring morning sun dazzled through the lace curtain in Rudro's bedroom. The bright light did not prolong his morning sleep, and he also remembered that it was a special day for him. His wife Priyanka was always early to wake up, therefore Rudro was not surprised to find the vacant space next to him in the bed. With a hesitant effort, he sat and looked outside the window. The nearby traffic added to the noise of the local area. Rudro had decided to take a day's leave from work on the request of his family members – his mother had pleaded for him to be at home on his 50th birthday.

After a quick shower, the youngest member of the family briskly walked down the polished staircase of the house which reached the living room. On the large sofa, Rudro's mother Sudha Devi sat with a beaded mala in her hand, saying her morning prayer as she looked at her son standing in front of her. As is the tradition of the Bose family, the family members pay their respect to their elders with a pranam on their feet after having a morning shower, which was a must for everyone. Rudro gently touched his mother's feet, and Sudha Devi blessed him with her right hand. She finished her prayers soon and fondly wished Rudro on his 50th birthday. In the meantime, Priyanka had brewed chai for the family, and they entered the south-facing dining room where the hot tea was served in dainty porcelain cups.

Sudha Devi sipped her tea and casually mentioned to her son – "this is a milestone birthday for you, Rudro. I have made special arrangements for you to celebrate the occasion," she finished her sentence with a sly smile on her face. Her youngest offspring was pleasantly surprised and felt reassured that the day's leave was worth the effort. His mother continued, "at midday, a masseuse will give you a body massage on the terrace; Priyanka has made arrangements on the porch for you. I am certain she will give you a good experience." Rudro was quick to pick up the word 'she', as it was customary for a masseur to give massages for male members of the family. Therefore, he was looking forward to the midday treat by a beautiful lady. For the next couple of hours, Priyanka and her mother-in-law were busy with household chores and frequently exchanged smiles in the kitchen. They maintained suspense. After breakfast, Rudro sat in the living room and read through all the newspapers which the maid had picked up from the front door.

The big grandfather clock in the hallway chimed at midday, and Rudro, with eagerness, asked Priyanka if he should go to the terrace. "No," said his wife, "wait, I will blindfold you and take you upstairs as if it is a surprise." Her husband was amused but agreed and wondered about the surprise. Priyanka gently tied a white cotton cloth on his eyes, and the couple slowly walked up the flight of stairs with Priyanka guiding the way. On reaching the terrace, Rudro felt the sun on his skin; Priyanka helped him to take off his kurta. She gradually helped her husband to lay on the large wooden bench on the terrace.

The front doorbell gave a shrill noise, and Sudha Devi instructed the maid to bring the guest in. Within a few seconds, an 80-year-old lady was ushered into the living room. The two elderly ladies exchanged a look and a grin, and Binodini was requested to go to the terrace where Rudro was waiting. A day before, she had visited the house and was instructed to give a body massage to Rudro on his 50th birthday as a special indulgence. Binodini knew of the plan for the day and was amused. She had travelled from a nearby town which was not known to the birthday man. On the terrace, Rudro waited patiently for his surprise "young beautiful masseuse." Priyanka and Binodini reached the portico and instructed Rudro not to remove the white cloth placed on his eyes until she returned.

The massage session began in all earnest. Binodini put some oil on her palm and sat on the small stool next to the bench and gently rubbed Rudro's upper body. For a few minutes, both Rudro and Binodini kept silent. After a while, Rudro spoke first, "Your hands are very soft; I can feel the muscles responding to the massage. You must be very experienced in this field, as I can sense a young expert pair of hands doing the rubbing." Binodini did not respond, but a big smile appeared on the lips which exposed the vacant space of the front three teeth. Rudro continued, "Something tells me that you are a young and beautiful masseuse." Binodini could barely hold on to a soft giggle, which was not heard by her client. At a distance and near the staircase, Priyanka watched in amusement and listened to her husband's comments. Rudro had an uncanny feeling that the lady did not want to pursue a conversation, so he stopped talking and hoped that his masseuse would do the talking at some point. But this did not happen, and after an hour, the massage session ended.

Priyanka walked back to the bench and unfolded Rudro's eyes. His first glance was at the elderly lady who stood nearby with a laughing look on her face. Rudro was slightly embarrassed, as he remembered his comments. However, he was more surprised than ashamed and, with deep gratitude, thanked Binodini for the invigorating massage. The elderly lady blessed him with a gesture and said, "I am not who you expected me to be, but I will give you a very good massage." Rudro smiled and asked her permission to inspect her hands closely. He thought to himself, as he saw her palms unfold, ***"Her hands are like rose petals, pink and soft, and they have not bristled with age; they are devoid of any blemishes or network of marks, the destiny lines are few and clear. The slender fingers defy age, and the nails are clear and bright – the touch of her hands felt like a soothing balm."*** Rudro looked at the lady again and said, "My surprise birthday gift will be cherished forever, as it made clear my perception about beauty and age. Thank you." Rudro paid his respect to the lady, and the three adults left the terrace to join the family downstairs.

****

Killing Machines

Six-year-old Fatima ran inside the house and shut the front door, shouting to other members of the household, "They are coming, they are coming." The child was in panic, scared and nervous, as her parents and family members gathered in the basement of the house. Outside, there were loud shouts and sounds of gunshots. People could be heard running frantically to hide from the onslaught of bullets that the foreign soldiers were firing indiscriminately. Within a short period, the chaos and bloody rampage was over, and the little hamlet of Hata fell silent – people were too afraid to step out of their houses to check on neighbours and friends. Ahmed, the patriarch head of the family, stepped outside the house, instructing other members not to follow him. The scene outside was one of complete carnage, with bodies of men and women strewn on the road. Fatima, a curious child and although afraid, disobeyed her grandfather's instruction and followed him outside, only to discover a bloody scene and dead bodies. As she observed the sight, she said in a sombre voice, "They are all dead, why did the soldiers kill them, Gadd?" Grandfather had no words of explanation, except to witness a mass murder of innocent and defenceless people.

In another land, the leaders had made up plans to wage war on a land in which Hata was a territory. Their argument to do so was drawn from a fear of invasion by the king of Hata. The leaders spearheaded a campaign of fear and imminent invasion by the King of Hata, claiming that he had built up stockpiles of ammunition to attack their land. Prior to the war on Hata and other villages, the leaders of the far-away land convinced their people that war was the only option to save the country. One leader was proactive in promoting his plan of invasion under the pretext of saving his country, and he had an ally in another country to support him. Oblivious to the plans of the foreign leaders and the country's imminent invasion, the tiny hamlet continued to live a peaceful life before the war. They tended to their livestock, and some villagers travelled to the nearby city to earn a livelihood. Hata was a village where many generations lived; there were very few signs of modern life. A few countrymen found the king to be despotic; however, the majority of the population were content with the way the country was administered. Oil was a major source of foreign income for the country and attracted the attention of the outside world.

The war waged by a foreign country continued for many months, and like Hata, other villages, towns, and cities were destroyed and razed to the ground. The massacre had left a permanent scar in the minds of many people. The country watched in silence and in horror the crimes committed by foreign soldiers, and its propaganda that weapons of mass destruction were built by the king to attack their land was the reason for the invasion. Many public figures and influential persons visited the land on many occasions to locate the weapons of mass destruction, but they returned to their country empty-handed. They had reported this to their leaders, but the personal ambition and power of certain leaders convinced the world that war was the only choice. Therefore, a bloody war was waged on the country.

A few years later, Fatima grew up to be a beautiful teenage girl pursuing college. She moved to the big city and, during her free time, she visited the old palaces and forts built by the murdered king of her country. Her childhood memory of carnage in Hata and the looting of valuables in the country by foreign militaries were etched in her mind. She had memories of her family's anxiety of living in terror in the village for as long as the foreign invaders were present. During family mealtime, Gadd would report about killing and pillaging in the country and the burning of buildings. There were also reports that valuables from the king's palace were plundered and transported in large ships to outside the country. The foreign soldiers patrolled the land, showing off their killing machines to instil fear in the minds of the people. The armies, on the behest of their leaders, had complete control of the land, and any unrest was quelled with gunshots and brutality. For many months, people lived in fear of their invaders; Hata was no exception, and on a cold winter morning, Gadd (grandfather) passed away, taking with him memories of a bloodbath, carnage, and decimation of his beloved country.

At the same time, the world woke up to a new era of false propaganda and aggressive persuasion to wage war on another country; leaders of such countries knew that the people must support their plans and decisions, therefore publicity was the right tool. However, thankfully, many practical people realised that war was not the solution to problems; invading another country solely based on individuals' whims and fancy and marketing of false alarm can do immense damage to a country and its people. The people of Hata would never forgive their aggressors. For

Fatima, the childhood experience would remain engraved in her mind for her entire life, for as an adult, she understood that the attack on her country was unjustified and cruel.

****

50

Three Sisters

Many years ago, a small kingdom in central India flourished under its popular and noble king named Pulak. The kingdom was known for its peaceful community and prosperity in the region. Its farmers and artisans were credited for bringing affluence to the land they had lived in for many centuries. The king was generous to his people and regularly held meetings in his large darbar (office) where matters of the land were discussed. His subjects had the freedom to voice their grievances without fear. Discourse about legal and economic matters was brought to the attention of the ruler, and answers to problems were sought from his advisory committee. The young king and his family lived in a large palace in the centre of the land near the river. The pink palace, built by his ancestors, boasted splendid rooms adorned with selected articles and mounted mirrors on the walls of many rooms. The king did not have any indulgence except to beautify his palace with exquisite ornaments he purchased from other lands.

Pulak's wife, Sujata, was elegant and beautiful. The couple had five grown-up children – three good-looking daughters, Rukmini, Radha, and Meera, and younger sons, Manu and Dhruv. The king was a loving husband and a devoted father. Rukmini was tall, slim, with pale skin and beautiful large eyes that stretched to their corners. Radha was of medium height, with pale skin, and her face also boasted a beautiful pair of eyes and a pointed nose. Radha's forehead was wide, often covered by a few strands of hair, which made her look more attractive. Meera's skin complexion was fair; she was the tallest of the three sisters, and her lips blushed pink. Her thick long black hair required attention from the grooming lady designated to look after the three sisters. The daughters' beauty and grace had reached far beyond the land. Pulak's children were home-educated by the best teachers of the territory, and the daughters excelled in the field of arts, while Manu and Dhruv were schooled in archery and the art of warfare. The kingdom was protected mainly by the trusted subjects of the king, who took over the baton from his father at the young age of 25.

For many years, there was peace in the kingdom, and no threats of invasion from neighbouring states were anticipated by the king. However, this changed when the Raja was made aware of plans by another king to invade the kingdom of Napur. Pulak initially did not take the threat seriously; however, within a few months, the fate of the kingdom changed permanently. Suddenly, one day, the king was faced with the reality of an approaching army of several hundred men mounted on horses, slowly making their way to invade Napur. The king quickly climbed to the terrace of his palace to observe the scene and directed his army general to prepare for war with the enemy. Pulak hurriedly went downstairs to his family and instructed the housekeepers to guide them to the inner chambers in the concealed basement for protection. Pulak's wife and children were ushered away from the palace to a place of safety, and the king stayed in the main palace room, ready for the ensuing battle. The gates of the palace were broken by the attackers, and a bloody battle followed for several hours. The king and his close aides gave orders to the army to fight valiantly to safeguard the land. The common people also joined the battle; however, many lives on both sides were lost. The scene in Napur was that of total carnage and devastation, with dead bodies casing the land. Many horses and elephants were also injured, and the combination of human and animal cries of agony could not be recognized, as their injuries were so severe.

In the meantime, in the hidden chambers in the basement, Pulak's family was anxious and wanted to know the fate of their king and the kingdom. Only a few people had access to the royal hidden chambers; therefore, any news from outside would be difficult. As night approached, the flicker of the oil burners in the large room revealed an anxious family. After a long battle of resistance, the invaders succeeded in entering the palace in search of the king to surrender. Pulak was seated in a room waiting for his enemy with a shining sword in his hand. He and his generals were ready for another dark battle in the palace. Pulak and his men fought bravely and succeeded in overpowering a few of the men. However, his generals were doubtful about the ongoing struggle with the enemy. One soldier, taking advantage of the bedlam and noise, slowly went to the king to advise him to leave the scene and disappear downstairs. However, Pulak was a proud king and a brave warrior; to abandon his people at the critical time would tarnish his image as a noble king. He continued to fight for his people and met every physical challenge with equal force and heroism. Unfortunately, outside and inside the palace, the brave king's army was overpowered late at night. Pulak was taken captive by the enemy, and a pall of gloom was cast over the land.

At the break of dawn, the fight for the honour of Napur was lost, and an eerie silence prevailed over the land. In the west corner of the palace, Pulak was seen sitting on his splendid chair, anxious about his family and his lost kingdom. The enemy had begun to search all the rooms in the palace in search of the king's family, in particular, for his beautiful daughters, whose beauty their leader knew about. The war was waged on Napur to capture and abduct the daughters and their beautiful mother and to loot the land of its wealth. This became more apparent as the army shouted and asked Pulak about the whereabouts of his family. Pulak remained silent and looked defiantly at his captor. He was also physically assaulted by a few soldiers when he refused to divulge any details of his family. The soldiers left the room in search of the family. After an hour, the king heard the familiar sounds of anklets coming from the marbled corridor. His worst fear had come true as he saw his family being dragged into the large chamber with their hands tied behind their backs. Manu and Dhruv tried to battle with the violent men; however, they were overcome instantly. Pulak looked on helplessly, unable to control his tears and anguish; his wet eyes revealed the emotions and internal turmoil of a lost king, husband, and father.

The aggressors waited for instructions from their king as they kept surveillance on the defeated king and his family. Rukmini, Radha, and Meera were scared and angry. However, they looked brave. The three sisters and mother looked at each other and then at their brothers and father. They were as helpless as their father, the king. News came soon that enemy king Kimchi was on his way to the palace to decide the fate of Pulak and his family. Everyone waited in silence for the arrival of the brutal king.

For Pulak, as king Kimchi entered the room, he looked in his sixties, oversized, greedy, and lecherous. He had a long thick moustache which covered most of his lower face and his lips. Therefore, when he spoke with arrogance, the hair on his upper lip did the talking. Kimchi looked at the young king Pulak with a sarcastic smile on his face, as if to say he had won his prize. The large figure approached Pulak and ordered him to give his daughters' hand in marriage and promised that the kingdom of Napur would be returned to him. The arrogant and lustful king also asked for Pulak's wife to be his concubine as Pulak was a defeated king and he had no right to have such beautiful women in his life. The young Pulak seethed with anger and hatred at the suggestions of the monster. He refused point-blank and said, "I would rather be killed than surrender to your lustful wishes." The argument and counter-arguments continued for some time. Nightfall was fast approaching, and Kimchi ordered the earthen lamps in the room to be lit by the domestics so that he could see the women. The maids did what they were ordered to do. Rukmini, Radha, and Meera looked at the earthen lamps lit – they were close to where they were standing. As if by telepathy, they read each other's mind and decided to do the unthinkable in the presence of all present in the room.

Rukmini realised the futility of the family's situation and fought with her jailor and freed herself; she ran to the nearest lamp and took the long scarf on her shoulder and put it on the fire; the cloth quickly inflamed and reached her body; seeing their older sister's action, Radha and Meera aggressively fought with their captors and freed themselves; they too sprinted to the nearest lit lamp and also inflamed their long scarves on their body. Within a short time, the three sisters' bodies were engulfed in fire; they were in excruciating pain as they shouted in chorus, "We will perform Sati rather than be the wife of a lecherous and wicked man; we will protect our chastity by doing this," and then they fainted in the room and soon died in pain. Their parents looked in grief and horror at their beloved children's joint decision to protect themselves from a cruel and sinful man. Sujata cried aloud, calling her daughters' names, and Pulak was numb with grief and sorrow and could not utter a word as tears of pain and loss covered his face. Manu and Dhruv covered their faces with their hands in humiliation, for they too could not protect their sisters. The wicked Kimchi witnessed the scene in horror and noted his defeat at the hands of three beautiful women; they were no longer his captors but free souls in pursuit of a dignified end to their life.

****

Crematorium

Supriya left her office early that day with the intention of taking a detour to a nearby town. The summer heat was intense, with a gentle breeze brushing her face. She stepped out of the office building and walked briskly to the bus stop, which was not crowded at that late afternoon hour. A few people were gathered under its shelter. The young woman boarded the bus, and her journey ended at Rampurhat. Supriya glanced at her wristwatch to keep track of time, ensuring she was not late returning home. She had forgotten to inform her mother of her plans for the evening, so she knew she had to be punctual, as her mother would be waiting for her return.

As a curious twenty-year-old, Supriya particularly enjoyed listening to ghost stories, a passion nurtured by her family's tales. It was no surprise that she wanted to experience the supernatural at a crematorium. She had heard stories about haunted houses, streets, palaces, and the crematorium she was visiting was the most talked about in the community. From afar, Supriya noticed the gates of the place wide open, with the gatekeeper sitting on a stool outside. She boldly approached the gates, attempting to enter the crematorium, but was stopped by the vigilant gatekeeper. "You cannot enter the shoshan (crematorium), and what is your purpose to enter this sacred place?" he questioned. Supriya, taken aback, replied, "I want to spend a couple of hours observing the last rites performed here; I've never visited a shoshan before and would like to see it firsthand." The gatekeeper, puzzled and bemused, said, "Women are not allowed entry into the shoshan, and secondly, people only come here with a dead body to perform the last rites. Therefore, you are not permitted to visit the place on these accounts, so please leave."

Undeterred, Supriya persisted in her attempt to gain entry. As darkness fell and no activities were underway at the shoshan, she unexpectedly offered the gatekeeper a hundred-rupee bribe. The gatekeeper, momentarily taken aback, quickly pocketed the money and allowed Supriya a brief entry, warning her not to be seen in any obvious spot within the crematorium. Supriya, without further challenge, stepped inside the crematorium.

With her saree neatly pleated at the front and her shoulder bag on the left, Supriya gracefully surveyed the forbidden place for a woman. The shoshan was empty, and at the far corner, she noticed three empty pyres, waiting to perform last rites for departed souls. Lost in thought, Supriya inspected the shoshan, noticing every detail. A few perennial trees had taken root, one bearing red blooms, which Supriya noticed in the onset of dusk. A wooden bench occupied a central position. As the evening sun set, the strange silence in the shoshan did not daunt the young visitor. She approached the pyres, captivated not by ghostly tales but by the peaceful and tranquil ambiance of the place. Far from the crowd, alone amidst the unknown journeys of the deceased, she felt a magical influence comparable to the Divine. Supriya's experience in the crematorium was one of bliss, peace, and tranquillity, a luxury in the big city.

The silence was suddenly shattered by footsteps and voices at the gate. Supriya turned to see a group of men entering the crematorium; four carried a dead body on a wooden khat. Overhearing their conversation about performing the last rites, her contemplation was interrupted by the gatekeeper's voice, "Madam, you have to leave now." Supriya, not daring to argue, left as quietly as possible to re-engage with the sounds and crowds on the main road outside.

Her bus journey home was delayed due to increased traffic. Supriya alighted at her home stop, but had to walk the distance to her house, as no rickshaws were available. While walking home, she opened her small umbrella as a light drizzle turned into a heavy downpour. Her home was at the corner of a narrow street, where a tall tree stood at the entrance. Approaching the tree in the darkness, she felt uneasy but not afraid. The tree cast a dark shadow on nearby buildings, and its branches swayed in the breeze. Supriya always tried not to think about the menacing tree in the darkness. Instead, she focused on the dinner awaiting her at home. Passing under the dark spot, she became more conscious of an unknown presence in the tree. She had experienced this before and had mentioned it to her mother. The tree was known to be haunted, but Supriya didn't let that affect her. She quickened her steps and often coughed aloud to announce her presence. Upon arriving home, she told her alarmed mother about her visit to the shoshan, and how the tree in the alleyway made her feel uneasy.

A few days later, as a cyclone prepared to make landfall over the Bay of Bengal, Supriya returned home early. After an early dinner, she heard the cyclone's howling sounds, closing doors and windows. At midnight, her family was rudely awakened by a loud crash. Not venturing to inspect the cause, they fell back asleep.

The next morning, the neighbourhood buzzed with activity around the fallen tree, struck by lightning during the cyclone. Supriya was relieved to see the end of the haunted tree, which had terrorised the community. The tree and its branches were cut and removed.

Years later, Supriya revisited the spot, now adorned with red rose saplings, stone borders, and a wooden bench. An elderly lady tended the plants daily, collecting the red blooms. Supriya's experiences at the crematorium and with the haunted tree had left lasting impressions about the mysteries beyond life, but she was also relieved that the haunted tree had met its fitting end.

****

Nitai

On a winter day when the sun was bright,
He set his feet outside in the light.
Nitai saw people outside his door,
Going about their business in awe.
With a smile on his chiselled face,
He walked towards the nearby lane.
His gait was of peace and tranquillity,
As he walked in harmony and divinity.

People had thronged the nearby river,
Bathing in the holy water.
Women offered prayers to their Deity,
And let the flowers float aloft.
The scene was quiet and deific,
For everyone seemed to be in worship.
Nitai sat under the nearby giant tree,
His eyes focused on the blue sky.
As His silence and presence
Attracted the attention of all persons.
They saw in Him a Godly light,
Shining from His body and might.
Nitai was silent and deep in thought,
For He knew his mission was God.
Mesmerised by His charm and beauty,
People sang in the chorus 'Nitai, Nitai'.

Their folded hands of worship lifted,
And broke the silence with songs of praise.
Nitai was in profound meditation,
And oblivious of the scene outside.
His body spoke of a saintly story,
To mark his journey towards eternal glory.
Only his smile revealed the truth,
And the worshippers understood the light
Of knowledge, peace, and love.

The voices raised in a feverish tempo,
Sang 'Nitai, Nitai' aloud with raised hands.
Believers danced around the tree,
In joy and love of the Divine.
Nitai was their ray of hope,
In a charred world of darkness,
And of love diminishing.
From far and wide, people heard
"Nitai, Nitai" song,
And they too joined the chorus
Of worship and sublime.
The morning glory was complete,
As worshippers and Nitai
Together they prayed for love and peace.

****

Sunset

Bhola worked in the local post office not far from the village. His family had lived in the tiny settlement for generations, and the young postman grew up amidst the natural beauty that was gifted to the hamlet. His family and extended family members were part of the local community, earning their livelihood by producing dairy products, growing and selling vegetables and fruits that grew in the large fields owned by their ancestors. Bhola and his two sisters studied in the village school and were skilled in the ancient Sanskrit language. Their parents were not keen for the children to go to the big city to pursue higher education; therefore, the family engaged in the business set up by Bhola's great grandfather. The only exception was Bhola, who convinced his parents that he would work in the post office. He was subsequently successful in passing the interview. Although his parents were not too keen, they relented to his wish, and Bhola was happy to be recruited as a postman, taking over the baton from his predecessor, Shambhu, who had reached retirement age.

For the young recruit, the day would start very early with morning rituals to follow, and he had to be at the post office before his manager arrived. Bhola was always punctual. Every morning, he would wait for instructions from his boss, collect the post from the box, and cycle his way through the villages to deliver letters. Families would wait anxiously to receive letters from their loved ones living in the city or other countries. This was the only form of communication with their relatives, so Bhola diligently delivered the mail punctually, even in adverse weather conditions. The post office had provided him with a new cycle with a small rack at the back and front to keep the waterproof post bags. On his short journey for postal delivery, Bhola would whistle or sing to break the monotony of the cycle journey. He would wave at people as he cycled through the narrow roads in the villages. Bhola was a familiar face, and the ring of his cycle bell would announce his arrival in the village. The residents looked forward to his daily visits. Sometimes he would be offered tea, which he politely declined, for he had the duty to deliver the last letter before returning home.

The postman's journey to work involved passing a small forest with tall trees and a narrow road. Bhola enjoyed the short cycle journey through the woodland every day. Sometimes he would see a few woodcutters in the jungle, and they would wave at each other as they passed by. The sun-kissed land would be swathed in green, and the birds would be happily singing their daily songs. Bhola would drink in the beauty of the morning glory before arriving at the post office, ready for his routine work. However, for Bhola, the return journey back home was a different experience.

In the sweltering summer heat, the postman would return home riding his bicycle, somewhat tired, but no less enthusiastic about the surrounding nature. Bhola would admire the evening sunset as it leisurely disappeared into the horizon, dazzling between trees, its rays shining on some leaves and carpeting the ground in a golden shimmer. The sunrays played hide and seek between trees and branches, and sometimes they briefly cast their spell on Bhola's face. As he slowly cycled his way, Bhola observed the fascinating ways of the sunset with awe and admiration. On one such evening, Bhola suddenly stopped in the middle of the road as he noticed a cow in the forest. Bhola had never seen an animal in the forest during his journeys, so he was surprised to see the lone animal. He parked his bicycle in a safe spot and walked slowly towards the cow; Bhola immediately recognized his neighbour's animal, which was lost but not confused. The docile white animal was standing facing the sunset as if it was also admiring its beauty and majestic appearance. The cow was not distracted by Bhola and continued to stare at the sunset with its wide black eyes. Momentarily, the animal looked at the playful sunrays tossing on the green leaves of trees. Bhola stood behind the cow silently as they both enjoyed the sunset with awe and delight. The peaceful surroundings provided them with the ambiance to enjoy the glory of creation and master the art of appreciation.

****